KEEKER

and the Crazy, Upside-Down Birthday

Series design by Kristine Brogno and Mary Beth Fiorentino.
Typeset in Weiss Medium.
The illustrations in this book were rendered in Adobe Illustrator.
Manufactured in China.

Library of Congress Cataloging-in-Publication Data
Higginson, Hadley.
Keeker and the crazy, upside-down birthday / by Hadley Higginson ;
illustrated by Lisa Perrett.
p. cm.
Summary: Catherine "Keeker" Dana decides to run away rather than give
up her beloved pony, Plum, when her parents suggest they will buy her
a bigger pony for her eleventh birthday, but an interesting new neighbor
girl might lead to a better solution.
ISBN: 978-0-8118-6256-1
[1. Ponies—Fiction. 2. Birthdays—Fiction. 3. Neighbors—Fiction. 4.
Vermont—Fiction.] I. Perrett, Lisa, ill. II. Title.
PZ7.H53499Kdt 2008
[Fic]—dc22
2007018700

10 9 8 7 6 5 4 3 2 1

Chronicle Books LLC
680 Second Street, San Francisco, California 94107

www.chroniclekids.com

KEEKER

and the Crazy, Upside-Down Birthday

by **HADLEY HIGGINSON**   Illustrated by **LISA PERRETT**

chronicle books · san francisco

Chapter

This is Catherine Corey Keegan Dana, but everyone calls her Keeker. Keeker is almost eleven. She lives in Vermont with her parents, five dogs, two cats, two horses, a goat, a bird, and a salamander named Solomon. She also has a pony, named Plum.

Plum is quite sneaky. But it's hard for her to out-sneak Keeker, who knows all of Plum's tricks!

In the fall, the leaves in Vermont turn all kinds of colors: red, orange, yellow, even purple. It's SO colorful, in fact, that people drive all the way up from New York and Boston to look.

Keeker's parents call the city people "leaf peepers." Often when Keeker and Plum are out riding, the peepers will drive by in a car, going very slowly. Sometimes they have cameras. They almost always have maps.

"Hellooooo, peepers!" Keeker usually says, giving them a little wave.

Plum prances a bit, to see if she can get into a picture.

Leaf-peeping season is fun, but it isn't the best thing about the fall. The best thing about fall is Keeker's birthday, which is in September.

Keeker's mom and dad like to surprise her for her birthday: Sometimes they plan a party.

Sometimes they whisk her away all by herself
to somewhere special. Keeker never knows
what's going to happen—but she always knows
it will be fun!

So fun, in fact, that Keeker starts bugging
her mom about it weeks and weeks before it
actually happens.

"MOM!" said Keeker three whole weeks before her birthday, "are we going to have a party this year? Are we going to go somewhere? Can I have a LOT of roses on my cake?"

"Oh, Keeker," said Keeker's mom. "It's too early to be talking about this! All I know for sure is that you're getting some new clothes. You're growing out of everything."

It was true; Keeker was getting very tall. All her pants were too short, and she had to keep making the stirrups longer on her saddle.

Even Plum could tell that Keeker was getting bigger. (Keeker's toes almost touched the ground when she was riding bareback.)

Plum pretended not to notice, though. She didn't want to hurt Keeker's feelings.

And in fact, Plum had plenty of other things to think about.

For one, the groundhog babies were all grown up—and they were very adventuresome! They kept coming into the barn to say hello, and Plum had to keep shooing them back to their own field. (Mr. Dana still didn't particularly like groundhogs.)

Pansy's foal, Rosie, was also getting bigger and bigger—and she loved to follow Plum! Every time Plum turned around, there was

Rosie, looking fuzzy
and curious.

"Hmmph," thought
Plum. "Silly little
baby horse."

But Rosie was so
cute. It was hard to
be annoyed with her.

Rosie also loved going out for rides.
Sometimes when Keeker and her mother went
riding together, Keeker's mom would ride
Pansy and lead Rosie on the lead line.

Occasionally, Rosie would get a little too
rambunctious (and skitter around and bump into
Plum), and then Plum would have to give her a
little nip.

Pansy didn't mind at all. She liked that Plum
was teaching Rosie to mind her manners.

Chapter 2

One sunny Saturday when it was particularly crisp and delicious outside, Keeker and her mom decided to go for a long trail ride.

"Let's leave Rosie at home this time," said Keeker's mom. "We'll put Goatie in her stall so she doesn't get lonely."

It was a good thing Rosie didn't come. They had gone only about a mile down the road when they ran into all kinds of commotion:

moving trucks and moving men and furniture
all over the place.

"Yippee," said Keeker's mom. "New people
are finally moving onto the Doolan farm!"

Mr. Doolan had decided he'd had enough
of the long, cold Vermont winters, so he had
moved to Florida. And now some new people
from Connecticut were moving onto the farm.

"That must be our new neighbor," said Mrs.
Dana, waving at a lady who was standing in the
middle of all the furniture looking miserable.

"Oh, hi," said the lady as she hurried over.
"Are you the Danas? We saw your horses when

we drove by. My name is Marcy Huffington.
That's my husband, Frank—" (Mrs. Huffington
pointed to a tall man near the house.) "And
that's our daughter, Zoe."

Zoe Huffington was very small. She was
wearing a striped dress and some wire bumble-
bee wings and was hiding her face behind a
stuffed bear.

"She's a little shy," said her mom. "Fortunately,
Brownie the Bear is very outgoing. . . ."

Mrs. Dana talked to Mrs. Huffington for
what seemed like forever.

"Mom," Keeker said finally, "we'd better get going. Plum is getting antsy!"

Actually, Plum was standing perfectly still. She was fascinated by the bee girl!

"That is one kooky-looking little girl," thought Plum.

The whole rest of the ride, Keeker's mom talked about the Huffingtons.

"I'm so glad they moved here," said Mrs.
Dana. "I can't wait to have them over for dinner.
And, Keeker, aren't you excited about having
someone to play with?"

"Sure," said Keeker, but inside she was thinking, "No!" The bee girl was obviously WAY
younger than she was. Keeker was almost
eleven, after all.

Apparently, Keeker's mom didn't care that
Keeker was too old to play with Zoe because
the next week she invited her over.

"Now, Keeker," said Keeker's mom. "I know

she's younger than you are, but her mom
said Zoe loves ponies more than anything. I
thought it would be nice if you would take her
out to the barn and introduce her to Plum."

"Okaaaaay," said Keeker.

When Zoe showed up, she was wearing her
bee suit again.

"Wow!" thought Keeker. "She likes costumes
even more than I do!"

Keeker put Plum on the crossties so she could show Zoe how a pony is groomed. But Zoe seemed almost scared of Plum. She peered at Plum while half hiding behind the stall wall.

"Well, ummm, OK," said Keeker to Zoe. "You don't have to come close if you don't want to. But here's how you do it. . . ."

Keeker picked up a currycomb and began rubbing circles on Plum's neck and shoulders.

Plum leaned forward on the crossties. "What a funny little girl! Why won't she come closer?" she wondered.

"Here, girl, girl, girl . . . ," thought Plum, trying to make herself look very gentle.

It worked. Zoe tiptoed up to Plum and kissed her lightly on the nose.

Plum was very surprised.

Keeker thought it was cute. "Awww," said Keeker. She smiled at Zoe and gave Plum a little pat on the neck.

Zoe and her mom stayed for lunch, and Zoe talked about ponies (and Plum) the whole time.

"SOMEONE sure had a good time," said Mrs. Huffington, smiling at Keeker.

After they left, Keeker's mom gave her a big hug. "That was nice of you to show Zoe a bit about ponies," said Mrs. Dana. "You ARE getting very grown-up!"

"Speaking of being grown-up," said Keeker. "What are we doing for my BIRTHDAY?"

Chapter

3

Keeker's birthday was only a day away now—
and Keeker was getting anxious! She'd seen
her parents whispering a lot, but they hadn't
asked her if she wanted to have friends over or
if she wanted to go roller-skating or anything.

Keeker had also already peeked in all the
usual present-hiding places—including in her
dad's workroom, in the barn, and even in her

parents' closet—and she hadn't found a thing.
There didn't even seem to be any wrapping
paper or ribbon in the house.

What was going on?

That afternoon Mrs. Dana came to talk to Keeker.

"Sweetie, you know you're getting taller, right?" asked Mrs. Dana. "And you know that Plum won't get any bigger?"

Keeker did not like the sound of this at all.

"Your father and I were thinking that it might be time for a new pony," said Mrs. Dana. "So, for your birthday—"

WHAT?! Had everyone gone completely bonkers? What about Plum? She LOVED Plum! She didn't want some stupid new pony!

Keeker did NOT want to have this talk!

"La-la-la-la-la-la-la-la!" Keeker shouted as she put her hands over her ears. Then she stormed upstairs and flopped on her bed. Her mom

hurried upstairs after her, but Keeker still didn't
want to hear about it. Keeker boohooed for
a while, but it didn't make her feel any better.
All she kept thinking about was the new pony
coming—and Plum leaving.

Keeker could think of only one thing to do:
She and Plum would just have to hide out for a
few days, until her parents came to their senses.

Keeker decided they would sneak away that
night, when everyone was asleep.

The whole rest of the day, Keeker pretended to be just fine about everything. She even pretended to be excited about a new pony.

But when no one was looking, she was very sad. She knew she was going to miss her mom and dad on her birthday, and it was probably going to be cold and yucky hiding out in the woods.

"I hope it doesn't take long for Mom and Dad to change their minds about Plum," she thought. "Maybe we'll have to stay away for only a day or two."

After dinner, when her parents were in the living room, Keeker filled up her lunch box with granola bars and cheese crackers and some green apples for Plum. Then she went up to her room and put all her warmest clothes in her backpack. She also grabbed some books and her flashlight.

But what about Solomon the salamander? He lived in a terrarium in Keeker's room. He liked to eat worms, which Keeker usually found for him. Who would feed him when she was gone?

Keeker decided to write her parents a long note telling them exactly where to find the worms and how many to give Solomon. She also reminded them that he liked lots of moss and that he enjoyed having his belly tickled.

Then Keeker found her sleeping bag (which was under the bed and covered with dust), and she began to wait.

She waited and waited. And waited!

When were her parents going to go to bed?
She thought she would just about die with
sleepiness.

Finally, they came upstairs. They were whispering a LOT, probably about Keeker's birthday.

That made Keeker sad again. For one teeny,
tiny moment, she wondered what the new pony
might be like.

But then she got mad at herself. Who cared
about the new pony! The important thing was

saving Plum. No one was going to take Plum away—not if Keeker could help it!

Ticktock. Ticktock. The clock next to Keeker's bed sounded very loud now that the whole house had gotten dark and quiet.

Keeker's parents had been in bed with the light off for at least an hour. It was now or never!

Keeker slipped out of bed (she was still wearing her clothes, of course) and grabbed her backpack, lunch box, and sleeping bag.

Then she tiptoed downstairs (making sure to skip the creaky step) and snuck out the front door.

Chapter 4

It was freezing outside! *Brrrrr.* Keeker had forgotten how cold it was at night in the fall. It was a good thing she had packed so many sweaters.

Keeker put her stuff in the barn, then went to find Plum.

Plum was fast asleep under her apple tree, having a wonderful dream about a sugar-cube

barn. She didn't want to wake up—even when she felt Keeker pulling on her forelock.

"Oh, this girl," thought Plum. She opened her eyes and there was Keeker, hopping up and down in the cold night air.

"Come on!" said Keeker. "We have to go!"

She slipped Plum's halter on, and they hurried up to the barn.

As it turned out, it wasn't so easy putting Plum's tack on in the pitch-dark.

"That is my NOSE!" thought Plum very crankily as Keeker fumbled around with the bit.

Finally, Plum was ready. Keeker tied her sleeping bag to the back of the saddle, then slipped on her backpack and hopped on Plum.

"OK," whispered Keeker. "Let's go!"

"Why are we whispering?" wondered Plum as she *clip-clopped* out of the barnyard. It was very, very dark.

"I can't even see my own whiskers," grumped Plum.

They made it out of the barn without waking up any of the other horses. Now they just had to get by the house.

"Let's walk on the grass so it's quieter," Keeker whispered, steering Plum over to the side of the road.

Plum always liked walking on the lawn. It was so spongy.

They walked along very quietly. No lights came on in the house. No dogs barked. They had just about made it past the house when suddenly—*CRASH!* There was a terrible loud clattering and clanging and banging.

"Yikes!" said Keeker.

"Help!" thought Plum. She backed up so fast she sat right down.

ALL the lights came on, all the dogs started
barking, and Keeker's mom came whizzing out
the front door with her bathrobe flapping (and
Keeker's dad right behind her).

Goatie was standing on top of the trash cans looking very pleased with himself.

"Oh, GOATIE!" said Keeker.

"Foiled again . . . ," thought Plum. Goatie always knew when someone was trying to do something sneaky (like the time Plum tried to hide in her pasture).

"Where are you going?" asked Keeker's mom.

Keeker jumped down and wrapped her arms around Plum's neck.

"I don't want a new pony!" said Keeker. "I like this one! Please, please, please, don't send Plum away!"

Keeker's mom and dad looked at her like she was nuts.

"Who said anything about sending Plum away?" said Keeker's mom. "Plum is staying right here! In fact, I was just talking to Mrs. Huffington about letting Zoe come over and ride, because Zoe is exactly the right size for Plum."

"Oh," said Keeker. That didn't sound so bad! And if Plum could stay, then maybe getting a new pony would be kind of neat.

Plum put her head down and began nibbling on the lawn. Of course she wasn't going anywhere! That Keeker was so silly.

Keeker and her mom put Plum back in her field, then went inside and made a big pot of cocoa.

"Feel better?" asked Keeker's mom.

"Yes, Mom," said Keeker sleepily. She did feel much better. Now that she knew for sure that Plum wasn't going anywhere, everything was OK again. And it was a big relief not to have to go camp out in the woods.

What a crazy, upside-down day!

Keeker went back upstairs and fell right to sleep.

Chapter 5

The next morning she slept late, and when she woke up, the house was very quiet. Keeker could smell good things coming from the kitchen, but she couldn't hear any talking. Everyone was outside.

For a few minutes, Keeker just lay there, enjoying the birthday-morning feeling. Then she felt something on the end of the bed. She poked around with her foot.

It was a halter! A BIG halter with a red bow tied on it and a shiny brass nameplate that said "Pebble."

Pebble!

Keeker heard a rumbling sound, like a big truck coming down the road. Could it be . . . a truck with a horse trailer?

Keeker flew out of bed and put her coat on over her pajamas and ran outside as fast as she could.

A horse van pulled into the driveway, and a dark-colored pony stuck his nose out the window. "Smells nice!" thought the pony. "I wonder where I am?"

They unloaded the new pony, and Keeker just stared. He was so big!

"He's almost horse size," explained Keeker's mom. "Pebble is a Connemara. They're one of the tallest pony breeds."

Pebble was a dark browny black color with a big white star in the middle of his forehead. He was very good-looking—even Plum thought so!

"Why, hello there," snorted Plum, sticking her nose over the fence to get a better look.

Just then there was ANOTHER rumble—another horse van was coming down the road!

"Here comes one of your party guests," said Keeker's dad.

In the front of the van, sitting next to the driver, was a spiffy-looking little girl who was waving hi to Keeker. Tifni!

"We thought a pony party would be fun," said Keeker's mom, giving Keeker a little smooch. "Happy birthday!"

Keeker couldn't believe it. It was the best birthday ever!

Tifni climbed down out of the horse van,
and she and Keeker danced around and
clapped and shrieked. (It was pretty exciting,
after all.)

"Girls!" said Keeker's dad when he couldn't
take any more shrieking. "Why don't you go
for a ride? Let's get your ponies tacked up."

"And get Plum ready, too," said Keeker's mom. "Zoe's going to come over, and I'm going to ride Pansy and lead Plum and Zoe on the lead line."

When Zoe came over, she wasn't wearing a costume. She was wearing proper riding clothes from head to toe. (She was even wearing a little tweed riding jacket!)

Plum stood very quietly while Keeker showed
Zoe how to use the horse brushes and put on
the saddle and bridle. Then Keeker and Tifni
got their ponies tacked up, and Mrs. Dana got
Pansy ready, and they all headed out.

Pebble *clip-clopped* along quite briskly.

"He's very forward," said Mrs. Dana, sound-
ing pleased. "He'll probably be a great jumper."

Keeker felt SO grown-up on her big new pony. She sat up extra straight and kept her heels down, just the way she was supposed to.

"What a delightful road," thought Pebble. "Listen to the birds! Look at all these trees!" He gave a little pull on his reins just to show how happy he was, and Keeker gave a little pull back.

After the ride, they had a pony tea party.
Keeker's dad put the picnic table under the
apple tree so each girl and each pony had a
place. Zoe and Keeker and Tifni had strawberry

cupcakes, and Pebble and Plum and Windsong
had some delicious fat apples.

That night Tifni slept over at Keeker's house.
Zoe went home with her parents and curled up

with Brownie and dreamed about Plum.

All the girls were snuggled in their beds. Out in the field, the ponies stood cozily nose to tail. The air smelled like wood smoke, and the stars dangled down.

It was a new season. A new school year. And just the right time for some brand-new friends.